THE PEPPERONI PALM TREE

BY AIDAN PATRICK MEATH & JASON KILLIAN MEATH

ILLUSTRATED BY KIRK PARRISH

To Ella & Andrew Enjoy! Jason

Fuze Publishing LLC

1350 Beverly Road, Suite 115-162 McLean, VA 22101

P.O. Box 3128 Ashland, OR 97520
www.fuzepublishing.com

Title art and layout design by Landis Productions, LLC

Printed in the USA

ISBN: 978-0-9849908-8-7
Library of Congress Control Number: 2012945588

"To Mom, Nini and Sonny and all the books and stories
you told and read." —Aidan & Jason

"To my parents, who always allowed me to set my own course.
And to the memory of my constant companion, Lucky.
The best dog anyone could ask for." —Kirk

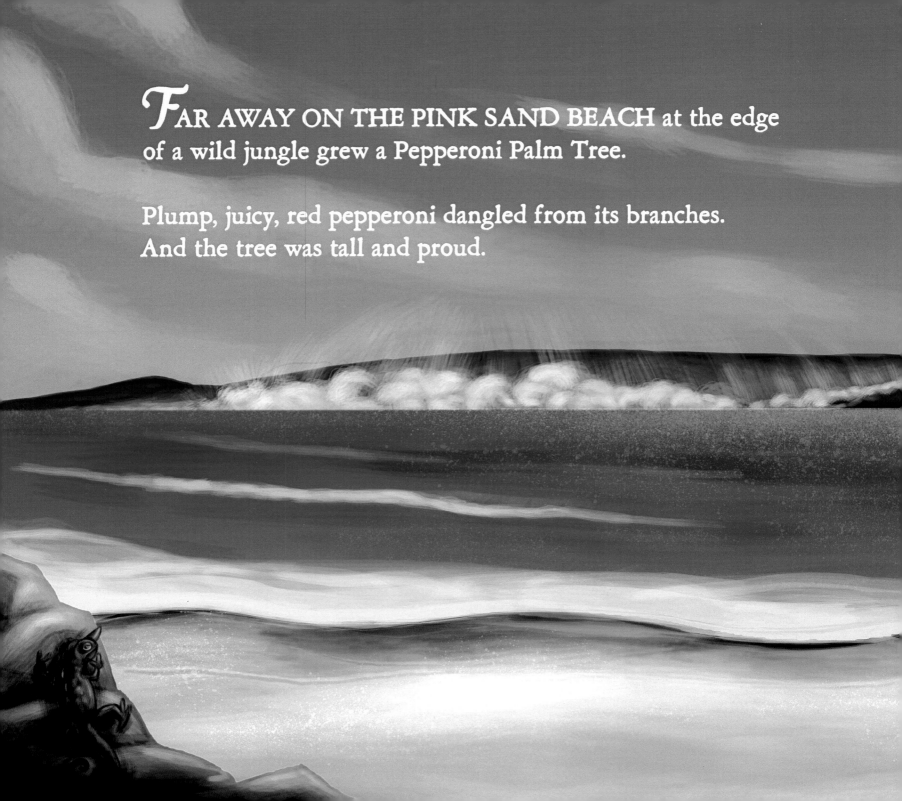

FAR AWAY ON THE PINK SAND BEACH at the edge
of a wild jungle grew a Pepperoni Palm Tree.

Plump, juicy, red pepperoni dangled from its branches.
And the tree was tall and proud.

The other palm trees snickered, "Where are your coconuts?
Palm trees around here grow coconuts."

The Pepperoni Palm Tree pretended not to hear.
He was certain there were more trees like him.
On some other island... someplace...

somewhere.

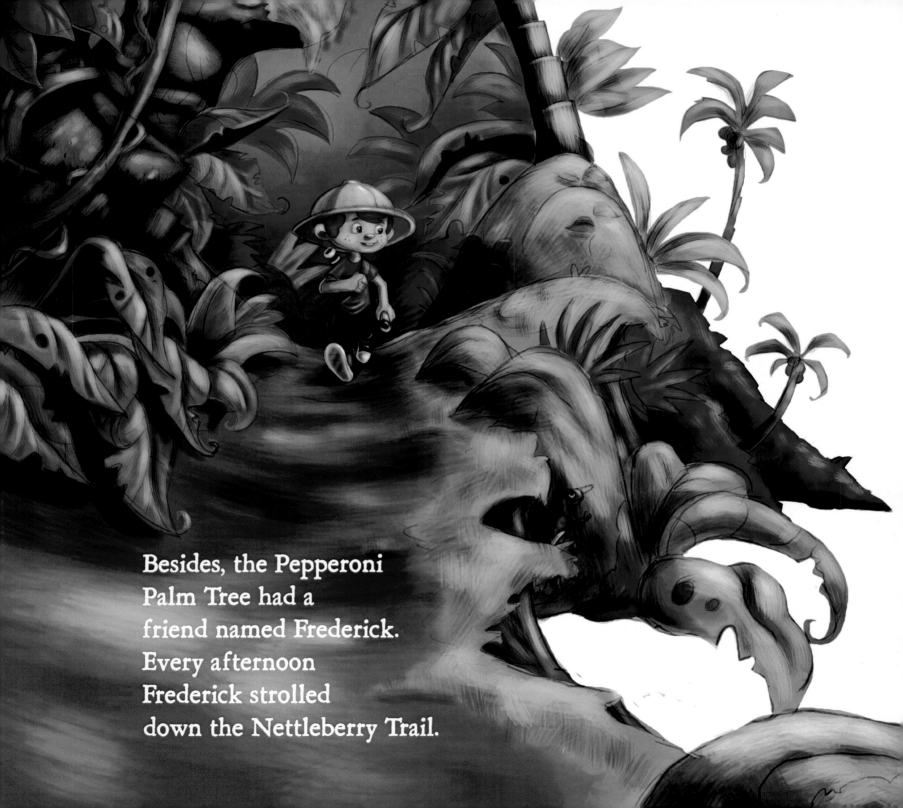

Besides, the Pepperoni
Palm Tree had a
friend named Frederick.
Every afternoon
Frederick strolled
down the Nettleberry Trail.

The tree stooped down to serve a snack of pepperoni.
"Deee-licious!"
Frederick said, smacking his lips.
"I have a hundred books about everything in the universe," he told the Pepperoni Palm Tree.

Nettleberry Trail

"Soon, I will find the book that's all about you." And this promise made the Pepperoni Palm Tree very excited.

"Pepperoni," sneered the prickly papaya plants, "does not belong on a palm tree."

But the Pepperoni Palm Tree remained cheerful. Frederick loved him, and he was sure to find out there were many more trees like him.

On some other island... someplace...

somewhere.

One day, Frederick pushed a great big box down the trail.

"The books about the universe!" the Pepperoni Palm thought.
"What do they say about me?"

Frederick started to read. He looked up once, then twice. Then, he read some more.

He read at night in the moonglow. He even read in a downpour!

When he turned the very last page of his very last book, Frederick sighed.

"Oh, phooey! You are nowhere to be found."

"But don't worry, Tree," Frederick went on. "I'm an ace explorer, and I will search near and far to find others like you."

Then he waved goodbye.

The next day, Frederick didn't come.

Weeks passed, then months. The jungle swallowed up
the Nettleberry Trail. "Where is Frederick?"
the Pepperoni Palm Tree worried.

"Will he ever return?"

"Ha! He isn't coming back," teased the banana bunches.
"Pepperoni on a palm tree — now that's simply bananas!"

Black storm clouds whirled over the choppy sea. A band of yellow-eyed monkeys danced up the Pepperoni Palm Tree singing, "We want coco-nuts, coco-nuts, coco-nuts!"

"That's a *pepperoni* palm tree," yelled the mango trees. "Too spicy, too smelly, not pretty and sweet like us."

Suddenly, a lightning bolt stung the Pepperoni Palm Tree,
and the monkeys let out a shriek and scampered away.

Later that night, everything seemed darker. The sun was on the other side of the world, and the soothing ocean breeze blew far away.

The Pepperoni Palm Tree felt alone.

Years passed with no sign of Frederick. The Pepperoni Palm Tree thought of his long lost friend every night. He hoped he was safe out there...

somewhere.

Then, one day a young man cleared his way through the overgrown Nettleberry Trail.

He carried a red toolbox.

The young man sampled a piece of juicy pepperoni.
"Deee-licious!"

It was Frederick, all grown up! The Pepperoni Palm Tree
was very excited.

"I have big plans for us," Frederick said, getting straight to work.

Frederick built a pizza parlor. Not just any pizza parlor —
a Pepperoni Palm Tree Pizza Parlor!

In no time, long lines of curious visitors stretched
down the sandy beach, eager for a taste of fresh
pepperoni palm tree pizza.

Word spread as quickly as the wind could carry it.

People all around the world heard about Frederick and his incredible Pepperoni Palm Tree.

"How is it possible?" the mangos muttered.

"It can't be so!" proclaimed the papayas.

And they bowed their branches and blubbered, "Boy were we a bunch of bamboo-brains!"

"You are the only one in the universe," Frederick marveled, "and that's what makes you so special."

Suddenly the trees started singing, "Pepperoni is great, pepperoni is grand, pepperoni goes best on our island!"

"Pepperoni pizza and a marvelous mango smoothie go well together too," thought the Pepperoni Palm Tree.

Frederick smiled knowing his friend was a cheerful, forgiving tree.

"Just imagine, we'll serve scoops of papaya and banana ice cream for dessert," Frederick exclaimed. "And don't forget coconut slurps!"

"Deee-licious!"

So it was that all the flavors of the jungle made the new pizza parlor a true wonder of the world.

The Pepperoni Palm Tree stood tall and proud once more. And the breeze lifted every branch skyward, to be kissed by the sun.

THE END

After Jason Killian Meath released his first book, "Hollywood on the Potomac,"
his son Aidan asked whether he could write a book.
"Sure," his dad said, "grab a piece of paper and get to work."
Aidan returned a short time later with The Pepperoni Palm Tree.

Once upon a
time there was
a Pepperoni palm
tree.

Acknowledgments

Very special thanks to the following friends:
Karetta Hubbard, Meg Tinsley, Molly Best Tinsley, David Landis,
Pamela Rytter, Julie Chlopecki, David Fuscus, Dave Swain, Scott Waz
and all the Griffins at Mater Dei School